Brooklyn Bailey,

BY Amy Sohn AND Orna Le Pape

THE MISSING DOG

ILLUSTRATED BY *Libby VanderPloeg*

DIAL BOOKS FOR YOUNG READERS

*For Emile and Yotam, my boys with the biggest hearts.
You carried us all with your love, optimism, and unshakable
belief that Bailey would find her way home.
And for Bailey, our hero.*
–O.L.P.

For my daughter, who loves her dog.
–A.S.

For Pam, Jon, and Erik.
–L.V.P.

DIAL BOOKS FOR YOUNG READERS
An imprint of Penguin Random House LLC • New York

Text copyright © 2020 by Amy Sohn and Orna Le Pape
Illustrations copyright © 2020 by Libby VanderPloeg

Visit us online at penguinrandomhouse.com

Library of Congress Cataloging-in-Publication Data is available.

The artwork for this book was created digitally.
Design by Jason Henry • Printed in China
ISBN 9780525552734 • 10 9 8 7 6 5 4 3 2 1

Monday started out like most mornings,
with Bailey the dog licking Yotam to wake him up.

Yotam got out of bed and took Bailey to wake up his big
brother, Emile.
Then they all went downstairs to eat breakfast with Ima.
They'd had Bailey almost a year, and she was Yotam's favorite.

He thought about her all day long.
He and Emile liked to roll around with her
on the rug and toss her the slobby pink ball.

Every morning after breakfast, before Ima and the boys
walked to school, Yotam and Ima would take Bailey to
Henry's Local.

Yotam would wait outside with Bailey while Ima ordered an iced latte.

Through the window Yotam saw his friend Mason, with Mason's mom, waiting on line. He wanted to say hi but he knew dogs weren't allowed in cafes, so he tied Bailey's leash to a metal chair.

He was just saying hello when he heard something outside.
A woman with a long coat brushed against Bailey's chair,
and Bailey JUMPED.

The chair toppled over with a CLATTER!
Bailey leaped at the noise and bolted down
the street, dragging the chair behind her.

CRASH

CRASH

Ima and Yotam raced outside after Bailey.
"Bailey!" Yotam shouted. "Come back!"
But Bailey didn't come back.

The louder the chair CRASHED, the faster Bailey ran, and the faster Bailey ran, the louder the chair CRASHED.

Bailey and the chair crossed Henry Street, weaving between cars.

Ima grabbed Yotam's arm and THEY crossed Henry Street, weaving between cars.

BEEP

YAP YAP

BANG

CLANG

Suddenly Yotam saw Bailey stop!
The chair had caught on a fence and Bailey couldn't run.
Trying to be quiet so he wouldn't frighten Bailey,
Yotam got closer, and closer...

But Bailey YANKED her pink harness from its leash—
and kept running.
She left behind the chair,
the leash,
and on the leash,
the ID tag with her name.

my name is
BAILEY
HELP ME GET HOME

Yotam picked up the leash and kept running.
At the hair salon, Bailey turned right. This was their street.
Maybe Bailey would stop. But she ran right past their building.

When they got to Court Street, a man with a big bushy beard said, "That way!"

A woman with a briefcase and a cell phone said, "That way!"

Yotam and Ima ran around the corner and all the way to the East River. "Have you seen a dog in a pink harness?" Yotam asked a man with ten cats.

He shook his head.

Yotam began to cry. "What are we going to do?" he asked Ima.
"Bailey's fast. She could be in Queens soon. If she gets that far,
she won't be able to smell her way back."

"But Bailey is smart," Ima said. "She'll figure out how to come
home."

She said that they should make a flyer, with a picture, in case
anyone saw Bailey.

At home they told Emile everything. Ima went driving in the car to look some more.

Yotam and Emile sat at the computer and made a MISSING DOG flyer.

Together they went to Cobble Hill Variety.

"Bailey's gone?" Omar, the shop owner, asked. "I can't believe it."

When Emile tried to pay him, Omar pushed his hand away.

"This one's free," he said.

On the way home Yotam and Emile put flyers
on every lamppost they passed.
    Bailey had been missing for three hours.
Where was she?

Was she fighting a pack of
rowdy strays in an alley filled
with garbage cans?
    He wished he could stroke
her golden fur and tell her
everything would be all right.

By the time Yotam arrived at school Mason had already told the class about Bailey running away. Yotam wished he'd never gone inside Henry's Local to say hi. If only he had stayed outside with Bailey!

"My dog Butternut went missing when I was your age,"
said Mr. Malament, "and he came back."
Izzie said, "I had a cat named Molly, and she was gone for
two weeks, but one day she showed up on the windowsill."

Yotam felt better.
Then Mason said,
"What if another family
decides to keep her?"
Yotam didn't talk
about Bailey anymore.

While the boys were at school, Ima spent all day hanging MISSING DOG signs, with the picture of Bailey in her pink harness.

Felicia, the mail carrier, said, "I'll hang one at the post office so the carriers on all the routes can see it."

Mike, a sanitation worker, said, "I'll announce this every day at roll call until we find her."

Around the corner from home Ima saw her friend Debbie, walking her turtle and pit bull. "I'll light a candle for Bailey in church," Debbie said.

That night Sapti and Grandpa came over to help. They made pizza for the boys while Ima went out to search.

Usually Yotam had three helpings of Grandpa's pizza, but tonight he could hardly taste it.

It was dark out. Where would Bailey spend the night? Would she climb a tree at the Prospect Park Zoo and sleep on a branch like a monkey?

It was late when Ima came back. Yotam was lying in his bed, awake.

"We should leave the downstairs door open," he said. "Then if Bailey comes back, she can get in."

"That's a good idea," Ima said.

She let Yotam go down to open it by himself.

He gazed out at the street. It was quiet, lit by the evening moon.

The next day, when Yotam came back from school, Ima said, "I got a call from a man who saw Bailey on Tillary Street! She was headed toward the Manhattan Bridge."

That made Yotam nervous. Tillary had three lanes of traffic on each side.

If Bailey tried to cross it . . . he didn't want to think about that.

"But she made it across," Ima said. "A woman called and said she saw her at Nevins and Degraw."

That corner was only a few blocks away from their building. Maybe Bailey was trying to come home!

The second night without Bailey, Yotam wanted to leave the door open again, but Ima said the neighbors might get mad.
In the middle of the night Yotam had a dream that Bailey was sitting on the front stoop, panting.
He decided to go downstairs, just in case the dream was real.
He thought he heard a clicking noise outside, but when he opened the door, there was nothing there.

The next morning, as Yotam stepped outside with Ima and Emile,
he saw a pile of poop right in the middle of the sidewalk.

"I think that's Bailey's," Yotam said.
"You're losing it," said Emile.
"It does look like hers," said Ima.
Yotam thought about his dream.

All day at school he stared out the window at the playground.
Where was Bailey?
Had she snuck on an F train to Coney Island to swim in the waves?

Sapti and Grandpa came for dinner again, and Ima went out on her bike.

At nine p.m., the phone rang. Yotam bolted for it.

"Someone just saw Bailey near Degraw Street!" Ima said. "Go downstairs right away!"

Everyone raced down the stairs—but Yotam was first.
He threw open the front door.

There was Bailey! She was panting. One of her paws was bleeding.

He wrapped his arms around her and held her by the harness so she couldn't get away.

Then Ima was there, climbing off her bike.

Everyone got together in a big, crying, laughing hug.

"I knew you'd come home," Yotam whispered to Bailey.

The next day after school Yotam went with Ima to the vet. Bailey had been gone for two nights and three days. She had lost seven pounds, and she had cuts on her paws, but she was going to be okay.

Yotam had an idea. They would have a welcome-home party for Bailey. He, Emile, and Ima walked all around the neighborhood replacing the MISSING DOG signs with BAILEY CAME HOME signs, inviting everyone to a party on their stoop.

There were treats for the dogs, and cupcakes and hot chocolate for the humans.

Bailey wore booties from the vet. Mike the sanitation worker came, and Felicia the mail carrier, Omar the shop owner, and Debbie with her turtle and pit bull. Mason showed up too.

"I guess she wanted to live with you after all," he said. While everyone was talking, Yotam held Bailey close. He would never know where she had gone those missing nights, but he knew where she would be sleeping tonight.

BAILEY